A
HARVEST
OF
CHANGE

40 short stories to inspire your self-improvement

NABIL N. JAMAL, PhD

PARTRIDGE
A Penguin Random House Company

To order additional copies of this book, contact
Toll Free 800 101 2657 (Singapore)
Toll Free 1 800 81 7340 (Malaysia)
orders.singapore@partridgepublishing.com

www.partridgepublishing.com/singapore

CONTENTS

Introduction

'*A Harvest of Change*' is a self-improvement book of forty short stories intended to help the reader see that things can be done differently, positively and creatively, to embrace change, and not give up in spite of all the negative influences that surround us.

'*The Second Harvest*', the sequel to '*A Harvest of Change*', is intended to further enhance the reader's self-improvement.

The sources that I used in researching the stories are: the internet, books, audio recordings, video recordings by renowned authors and speakers, even cartoons, and of course my very own material, all of which are credited at the beginning of each.

Being a performance development facilitator by profession with extensive experience in the field, I use many of those short stories in my sessions to deliver the desired performance changes in participants, very successfully.

People love short stories and associate with them, and a lesson can be better accepted if it is derived from a story; and as such, I believe that anyone, 18 years and above will enjoy reading this book and find benefit in the process.

Acknowledgements

I would like to thank the following people who have helped bring my two books into fruition.

Publisher's Assistant: I would like to start by thanking *Shelly Edmunds* (Publishing Service Associate) at Partridge Publishing, who has helped my two books move very smoothly from one phase to another throughout the publishing process.

Artwork: I would also like to thank the artists who participated in hand-drawing the sketches that you see in my two books, *'A Harvest of Change'* and *'The Second Harvest'*; namely, *Nancy El-Fata,* fifty sketches; *Yvette Ohanian,* twenty nine sketches; *Ali Callanta,* one sketch, and my brother, *Sany Jamal,* one sketch. All other images were made by me.

Drive to Completion: A very special thank you goes to my good friend, *Ghassan Khairallah,* who kept after me until I finished my first book, *'A Harvest of Change',* and who also introduced me to *Partridge Publishing.*

Finally, to *my family* who has adopted my positive habits, I thank you all for the unwavering group momentum that kept me going until I finished both books.

Leg of Lamb

Story Source: *Zig Ziglar: "Goals"*

Shortly after their return from honeymoon, and as her husband was preparing to leave for work, the bride asked him to buy a leg of lamb for her to roast, and also to remember to ask the butcher to chop off the bone extruding from either end of the meat.

Her huband was curious and asked why this should be done.

The wife answered that her mother taught her to roast a leg of lamb that way.

So he commented that his mother had roasted many legs of lamb in her lifetime, but has never chopped off the bone on either end, so what purpose does it serve to chop it off?

Naturally, the wife was not happy at his comparing his mother to hers, "Here's the phone, why don't you ask my mother directly?"

So the husband did just that, he called his mother-in-law and asked her why she chopped the bone extruding on either end of the leg of lamb.

His mother-in-law answered that her mother (the bride's grandmother) had taught her to roast the leg of lamb that way.

So he asked her if he could ask the grandmother (who was living with her), so the mother passed the phone on to the grandmother.

So he asked the grandmother the same question.

The grandmother drifted in her thoughts for a minute, then answered: "When I was a young bride, over 60 years ago, my husband bought me my first cooker, but it had a small oven compartment, and a whole leg of lamb just couldn't fit in it; and so, I would ask him to have the extruding bone chopped off on either end of the meat at the butchers', so I could fit it in my oven."

The Takeaway: *The bride's grandmother had a genuine reason for chopping off the extruding bone on either end of the leg of lamb.. 60 years ago.*

The bride's mother applied what she saw her mother do (without asking why), although by the time she got married, her cooker would have had a very big oven compartment that could fit a whole lamb.

The bride also applied what she saw her mother do (without asking why) although she too must surely have a big cooker.

Had it not been for the curiosity of the groom to ask Why?, the bride would have surely taught her inherited method of roasting a leg of lamb to her daughters in the future.

Critical thinking makes us question things that we see as strange, illogical, incompatible, odd, could be done differently, hasn't been done before but could be, etc., because . . .

a. *Things that apply to others may not apply to us.*

b. *Things that were applicable in the past may no longer be applicable today.*

c. *We are not satisfied with the reasoning of what we are told.*

And the list of triggers that could initiate your questioning process is endless.

Ask yourself this sequence of questions if you believe things should be changed:

1. *Do things really have to be as they are currently?*

2. *What would you change?*

3. *Is your proposed change physically and financially doable?*

4. *Most importantly, can you influence others to support your proposed change?*

Two Statistics Problems

Source: *Wikipedia: George B. Dantzig*

George B. Dantzig (1914-2005) is renowned as the father of "Linear Programming".

While he was a graduate student at UC Berkeley, age 25, an event in his life made him very famous.

One day, Dantzig arrived a bit late to his Economics class, and he noticed two statistics problems written on the blackboard. Assuming they were a homework assignment, he copied them down. According to Dantzig, the problems "seemed to be harder than usual", but a few days later he handed in completed solutions for the two problems.

Six weeks later, Dantzig received a visit at home from his Economics Professor, *Jerzy Neyman*, who was both excited and eager to tell him that the problems that he had solved were two of the most famous *unsolved* statistics problems ever.

Had Dantzig been present in the class when Professor Neyman announced the impossibility of solving those two problems, he would have been influenced by the negativity of the professor's words and wouldn't have bothered to try to solve them.

Dantzig's story quickly became urban legend, and continues to be used as a motivational lesson demonstrating the power of positive thinking.

The Takeaway: *Why was Dantzig able to solve two problems that the greatest statisticians found impossible? Positive thinking always helps us find solutions, while negative thinking inhibits our trying, calls on us to resign/ give up, and not believe in our capabilities.*

Chain and Peg

Source: *the internet*

Do you know how they keep a tamed elephant from running away? They tie a chain around the mighty elephant's leg, and pin it to the ground with an iron peg. The 10-foot tall, 5-Ton hulk could easily snap the chain, uproot the peg, and walk away; but it doesn't even try to. The world's most powerful animal, which can uproot a tree as easily as you can break a toothpick, remains tied down by a relatively flimsy chain.

How come?

When an elephant is a baby; its owner would do exactly the same thing - one end of a chain tied around its leg, and the other end to a peg in the ground. The chain and peg are strong enough to prevent a baby elephant from breaking away; and soon, the baby elephant would stop trying to escape. As a big elephant, it remembers its baby-limitations that it can only move as much as the chain will allow. It does not matter that the 100-kg baby is now a 5-Ton powerhouse, for the big elephant, *the only* limitation it now has, is in its own mind.

The Takeaway:

1. *Humans are like big elephants; we all have that incredible ability to achieve almost anything we set our minds to; and yet, like big elephants - in certain matters - we have our own chains and pegs, our self-limiting beliefs that hold us back. Sometimes, it is a bad childhood experience, a one-time failure, or something preventive that we are told that couldn't or shouldn't be done - all of which frighten us from trying.*

2. *We also get used to doing things in a certain way because we tend to believe it is the correct way to do it, so why reinvent the wheel, why change? And yet, with time, many things do change, and what was doable in the past may no longer be doable today. Many people will embrace the change, and if we do not follow suit, we may lag behind and miss-out on new opportunities.*

Here is a classic example why people embrace change with time: Communication between banks.

- *In 1750, instructions sent via horseback couriers.*
- *In 1812, instructions sent via homing pigeons.*
- *In 1910, formal instructions sent by plane/car, and informal ones via telephone.*
- *In 1960, formal instructions transmitted via telex.*
- *In 1980, supporting documents transmitted via fax.*
- *In 2005, formal instructions via high-speed, encrypted, dedicated internet.*

Ask yourself, what is holding you back, what is your chain and peg? Don't you think you owe it to yourself to find out if doing something differently can be better than how you are currently doing it?

Break the shackles of your bad experiences, the negative influences of others, and your own self-limiting beliefs. Set yourself free to try; it is possible that you may fail, but then, if you do not try, you will never know what you might achieve.

3. *Unfortunately, the problem is deeper than this. In life, we often play the role of the owners of baby elephants - as parents, teachers, colleagues and friends. When that happens, remember to handle your baby elephants with care, not to be overly critical, and to loosen the chain to allow them a chance to think for themselves and try!*

Marching the U.S. Infantry

Source: *The internet.*

As stated in the U.S. Army Field Manual 21-18 - Procedures and Techniques of Foot Marches, and unchanged from the days of the U.S. Civil War until recently, the manual calls for marching general infantry (GI) units for eight hours non-stop, with the purpose of training them to cover long distances on foot.

But this has now changed, the US Army marches its GIs for fifty (50) minutes and allows them to rest for ten (10), and repeats this for each of the mandatory eight (8) hours.

The reason behind this change is that one training officer was able to prove by physical experiment that in doing so, soldiers were able to cover more distance, arrive at destination faster, and without being exhausted.

The Takeaway: *Have you ever considered changing the routine of any of your tasks? Think positively, think differently, think out of the box, and you may surprise yourself in identifying new, more efficient ways in doing things. Just think.*

Flea in Glass

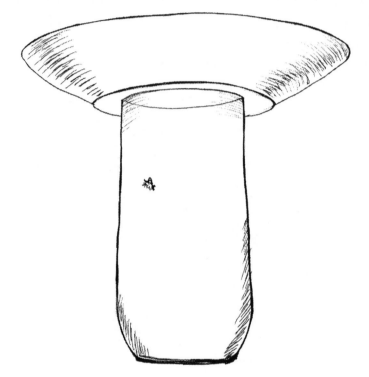

Source: *Several sources on the internet and Wikipedia.*

Jean-Henri Fabre (1823-1915) is considered the father of modern entomology (the study of insects) for his numerous findings in the field.

In the early 20th Century, Professor Fabre conducted an experiment on the height of a jump of a flea. He placed a flea in a 10cms drinking glass, and the flea easily jumped out of it. He repeated the experiment several times, and the flea would invariably jump out of it, i.e. it was capable of jumping higher than the 10cms tall glass.

He placed a ruler behind the glass and measured that the flea was reaching a height of 13cms every time it jumped out of the glass.

Then Prof. Fabre covered the glass with a plate, and observed.

As the flea continued its endless attempts to jump out of the glass, it would bang into the plate and Professor Fabre would hear a tiny thump upon impact.

Prof. Fabre then left this experiment for other experiments. When he returned to it, he noticed that the flea continued to jump, but now there was no thump (impact noise). Upon closer observation, he noted that the flea was not hitting the plate in its jumps anymore.

He removed the plate, and to his astonishment, the flea was still jumping but not high enough to clear the 10cms mouth of the glass.

What happened to the flea?, he wondered, *before covering the glass with the plate, it was capable of jumping 13cms, and after the plate was introduced it was not even clearing 10cms?*

He concluded: Before imposing this external limit (the plate) upon the flea, its capabilities were open, it easily cleared the 10cms glass. After the introduction of this external limit, the flea applied its own self-limit on its jump to be _within_ the external limit (it controlled its jump to be just less than 10cms); the flea had actually conditioned itself to jump so high only.

His analysis: Considering the relatively high speed of impact to the size of the flea, banging into the plate repeatedly must have been quite a painful experience. The flea still wanted to escape from the glass, but as it approached the plate it would remember the pain, and time after time, it controlled its jump not to bang into it.

**The Takeaway**: The same thing applies to people, they get conditioned that they can do so much only within the limits enforced upon them - they work within those external limits.

Each of us is born with unlimited potential, which we soon relinquish most of, as we accept the enforcement of external limitations on our actions. Fear of punishment (loss or pain) would deter us from trying to challenge those external limitations.

1. _Your parents are the first to set guidance limitations for you; such as tidying up your room, finishing your homework, doing chores at home, not hitting your little sister, and if you disobeyed, you would be punished._

2. *Then come laws and regulations (civil / social / governmental / judicial) that are commonly set for all people in society; such as import regulations, building codes, traffic laws, etc.; such limitations are for our benefit because they organize all our actions in the community.*

3. *Then come individual rules and limitations..*

   a) *Some, that you do accept and allow to influence you (friends, classmates, teachers, co-workers, managers . . .); in general, their influence would benefit both, you and they.*

   b) *Some, that you do not accept, the rules and restrictions that you feel are wrong, outdated, unjust, unfair, or illogical; those that you are not happy to have forced upon you. Considering your circumstances, this is where you decide to accept their control or to confront them.*

   A very good example of this is the rise of the Nazi Party to power in Germany in the 1930s. In its early days, most Germans felt that the Nazi Party was too small to bother about; but then the Party grew very powerful and made it a point to control everything; it was then too late to confront them, and the German people were obliged to accept the serious indoctrinations and restrictions that the Party enforced.

Ask yourself, what will you do if you are faced with a similar situation? Will you remain quiet as others slowly get to control your freedom of choice, or will you stand up to them before it's too late to do anything about it?

Processionary Caterpillars

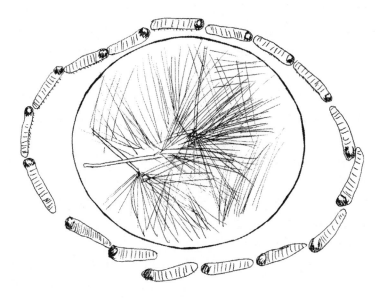

Source: *Several sources on the internet.*

In another famous experiment conducted by Prof. Jean Henri Fabre, he lined Processionary Caterpillars *(they are so called because they follow each other like a train)* in a circle around a small plate in which he put their favorite food, pine needles. The caterpillars smelled the food and started following each other around the plate without stopping for 7 days - each following the one in front of it thinking that it knew the path to the food, until they eventually dropped dead from starvation and exhaustion.

With their favorite food less than an inch away, they starved to death. Those caterpillars were very active, but their efforts did not benefit them, they lacked direction, they did not reach the food. *Because there was no direction, they "confused" their activity with accomplishment.*

A lot of people live their lives this same way - *no direction.*

Look at this real example: Two salesmen, with the same salaries, commissions and benefits, having the same educational background, years of experience in the field, selling the *same* products, for the *same* employer, and operating in the *same* area, and yet, one is doing very well and the other is not doing well at all. How can this be? Two reasons: (*a*) their way of *thinking* and (*b*) their *direction.* Many people are hyper, hard-working and always busy. But at the end of the day you will see no evidence that they've accomplished much because *they lack direction.*

The Takeaway*: This story addressed falling into endless routine, the need to review it to see if there is need to modify it.*

Changing your routine: Most of us are accustomed to routinely perform daily tasks without giving them any thought (e.g. washing up, getting dressed, driving in traffic to work, spending 8 hours at work, driving back home again in traffic, TV dinner, then sleeping).

If we study the above routine, we find that some of its steps may have lost their effectiveness with time. For example, getting stuck in traffic while going to work; if we changed something simple in one of those steps, like leaving home 15 min earlier, or taking a different route, we would have avoided a frustrating traffic jam.

1. *So, ask yourself about each of your daily routine tasks (personal, work and social):*

   a) *Does this routine deliver the same results today as it did long back? (i.e. Is there need for a change in the routine?)*
   b) *Is this (specific) step in the routine really necessary? Could I skip it?*
   c) *Must I do it this way? Is there an easier way to do it?*

2. *Following others: Many of us follow somebody blindly (e.g. a political leader) as in the story of the Processionary caterpillars mentioned above. Ask these questions to decide on what benefits you:*

   a) *Am I doing right in following this person? Do we share a common goal?*
   b) *Is he the correct leader for me to follow?*
   c) *Does he really know how to achieve our common goals? Are we on the right path?*
   d) *Are there any doubts that he may be working for his personal gain only?*

Kohler's Chimp Cage

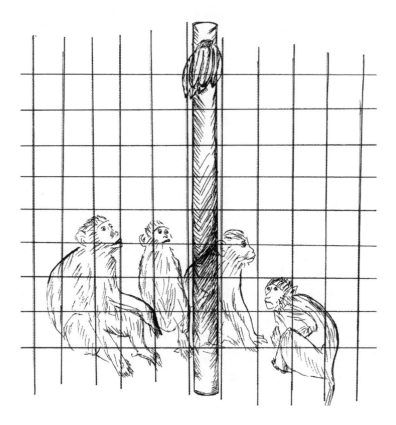

Source: *Several sources on the internet and Wikipedia.*

Wolfgang Kohler (1887-1967) was a German psychologist and phenomenologist, who was famous for his insight learning tests on chimpanzees.

In 1944, Kohler built a special monkey cage fitted with a network of showers attached to its ceiling that were connected to a trigger fitted to a vertical pole in the center of the cage. He then hanged a bunch of bananas on the trigger, such that if a chimp tried to pull down a banana, the trigger will activate all the showers to rain cold water everywhere in the cage.

Kohler placed 4 chimps inside the cage. As soon as one of them became aware of the bunch of hanging bananas, it quickly climbed the pole to reach it, as soon as it pulled on a banana, cold water showered all over the cage rendering all chimps drenched with water.

The chimps quickly cuddled together in a corner, shivering with cold (chimps hate bathing, so how if it were cold water?). Kohler turned the showers off.

A few minutes later, the same chimp again attempted to take a banana, and the punishment was instantly repeated. After several attempts by other chimps, they all came to understand that the cold shower was a punishment whenever a banana is touched. So they stopped all attempts to take a banana.

Kohler took one of the chimps out of the cage and introduced a new chimp. As soon as this new chimp saw the bunch of bananas and tried to ascend the pole, the other chimps from the original control group instantly attacked him, pulled him down and hit him, explaining the punishment in chimp language.

After a short while, Kohler took out a second chimp from the original control group, and brought in a second new chimp to the cage. As soon as this new chimp saw the bunch of bananas and tried to ascend the pole, all the other chimps pulled him down and explained the matter to him.

After a short while, Kohler took out a third chimp from the original control group, and brought in a third new chimp to the cage. As soon as this new chimp saw the bunch of bananas and tried to ascend the pole, all the other chimps pulled him down and explained the matter to him.

After a short while, Kohler took out the last chimp from the original control group, and brought in a fourth new chimp to the cage. As soon as this new chimp saw the bunch of bananas and tried to ascend the pole, all the other chimps pulled him down and explained the matter to him.

We note the following:

a) None of the original control group remained in the cage (the ones that actually experienced the cold shower punishment).

b) None of the chimps now in the cage (a second group) experienced the cold shower punishment, and yet, they were influenced by the original control group, and as a result, none dared to climb the pole to get a banana.

c) Finally, Kohler never intended to punish this second group with cold showers if any of them attempted to take a banana; amazingly, none of them tried.

The Takeaway: Fear is our biggest enemy. Many people do things in the traditional manner out of fear of punishment; they put on their car safety belt, not out of conviction, but out of fear of getting a traffic violation (a ticket); they follow an autocratic leader (manager, president, kingpin,..) out of fear; and as long as fear resides in their minds, they will not oppose that leader; and finally, many will base their actions on what they are told by others to be right or wrong, doable or not doable, <u>even if</u> those people never really experienced it.

I call on you to be brave, to start thinking for yourself, to question all the things that are being forced upon you. You may not have many options right now, but you <u>always</u> have the final say (regarding yourself only). Assess the consequences of your options, and decide on one.

Bannister's 03m, 59s, 4/10

Source: *Several sources on the internet and Wikipedia.*

Roger Bannister is the most celebrated English athlete alive today, best known for running the distance of a mile in less than 4 minutes. This story conveys what made him so famous.

It was common knowledge (and wrongly so) until 1954, that it was impossible for the human body to endure running the distance of a mile in 4 minutes. Doctors had unanimously agreed that blood capillaries (small veins and arteries) would explode and accordingly, the human heart couldn't possibly handle the resulting huge pressure. Likewise, sports instructors and physiotherapists unanimously agreed that the human leg muscles couldn't handle the extra movement needed to cover that distance in 4 minutes.

Let us look at the above statements with logical, unbiased examples: if a fat man weighing 100kg were to run a mile, it would take him almost 20 minutes to do so. And if a thin, non-athletic young man weighing 60kg were to run that distance, it would take him about 10 minutes. But the fastest of professional athletes (in 1954) was able to run that distance in 4 minutes, 30 seconds; and this was what confirmed the impossibility of running a mile in 4 minutes flat.

Then came Roger Bannister, an English athlete who could not accept those medical and physical assumptions, and dared to challenge them in 1952 that he will run the mile in less than 4 minutes; he intensified his training, among which leg-stretching exercizes, and underwent a very special diet to go with it before he confirmed he was ready for the challenge.

The historic event took place on 6 May 1954 at Iffley Road Track in Oxford; it was watched by over 3,000 spectators; and Bannister was successful in running the mile in *under 4 minutes* → *03m, 59s, 4/10*. This groundbreaking event earned him world fame as the first athlete to register two great records: beating the previous 1 mile record by an unbelievable 30 seconds, and crushing the wrongly upheld belief of the *"impossibility"* of running a mile in 4 minutes.

Ever since Bannister's 1954 great accomplishment, more than 5,000 athletes have broken *his* 1mile record. How could this happen, before him it was an *impossibility*, and after him it became *easy*?

"Here's how man thinks, if no one's done it, why should I try? It's a waste of time; but if he can do it, I can do it better". - Nabil N. Jamal

The Takeaway*: Most of the human race have been programmed over generations that certain things are de-facto - must be taken for granted. Only those who question those imposed ideas, believe in their capabilities, and dare to challenge those ideas, are capable of changing those beliefs forever and acquiring the fame and glory that go with it.*

High Jump Flop

Source: *The internet.*

Dick Fosbury is one of the most influential athletes in the history of track and field; he revolutionized the high jump with his unique technique, and has since presided over the World Olympians Association for a number of years.

At the 1968 Olympics in Mexico City, Dick Fosbury took the gold medal in the high jump and set a new Olympic world record at *2.24 meters*, displaying the potential of the revolutionary *new* technique that he had invented and dared to use - *jumping backwards* - unlike all others who jumped forward.

From that day onwards, the *"Fosbury Flop"* (jumping backwards) became the standard for the high jump event, and is adopted by the majority of high jumpers today.

The Takeaway: *Need is the mother of invention. Fosbury was seeking ways to improve on the height that he was attaining in the high jump, and discovered that by jumping backwards he could clear the bar at higher levels than jumping forward. He practiced it continuously until he mastered it.*

If one thinks differently (out of the box), sees the value of his "new" idea, tests out its feasibility first, then dares to perform it publicly, his success will be highly rewarded.

But there are times when such persons are over-enthusiastic, that they skip testing out their idea, and fail in its public performance. I highly recommend to always test one's ideas first.

1492: A New World

Source: *the internet.*

Christopher Columbus (1451-1506) was an explorer, navigator, colonizer, and the discoverer in 1492 of what was then known as "The New World".

Columbus was one of the few who believed in Galileo's theory that the world is spherical, and not a flat surface;

most people believed that the world ends at the horizon after which there is a steep fall to hell. Until Columbus, no one dared to venture far from known shores.

1485 - Portugal: Columbus first proposed his plans to search for a western route to China and India by sailing west, to Portugal's King João II. The Mediterranean Sea was then the only route used by European merchants in their travels to the Orient to import silk, rice, and spices. The King submitted Columbus's proposal to his experts, and it was *rejected* because in their opinion Columbus underestimated the travel distance as 3,860km; and their opinion was right, it turned out to be much more, but there was no way to find out for sure except by physically sailing West into the unchartered Atlantic ocean.

1486 - Spain: Columbus presented his plans to Spain's Queen Isabella, who in turn, referred it to a committee that rejected the idea as *impractical.*

1486 - England: Columbus dispatched his brother Bartholomew to King Henry VII of England, to inquire whether England might sponsor his expedition, but also *without success.*

1488 - Portugal (second time): Columbus again appealed to Portugal's King João II. This meeting also proved unsuccessful as the King believed it to be a *far-fetched project.*

1488 - Genoa and Venice: Columbus approached the courts of both, Genoa and Venice, but *none encouraged* him.

1492 - Spain (second time): After continually lobbying at the Spanish court for two years, Columbus finally succeeded in convincing King Ferdinand and Queen Isabella, who in turn agreed to Columbus's terms that if he succeeded, he would be given the rank of *Admiral of the Ocean Sea*, would be also appointed *Viceroy* and *Governor* of all the new lands he could claim for Spain, and would be entitled to *10% of all the revenues* from the new lands for himself and his descendants for eternity, plus many other great benefits. His son Diego later wrote: the Royals did not really expect him to return, let alone to succeed.

The Royals saw the potential, however remote, of gaining the upper hand over rival powers in the contest for the lucrative spice trade with Asia. Their investment in three ships was minimal compared to the expected gains if Columbus pulled through.

Columbus sailed with the three ships (that became the most famous in marine history), Niña, Pinta and Santa Maria, from the seaport of Palos; and on 12 Oct. 1492, 33 days after facing high seas and depressed and scared sailors fearing the unknown, they landed on an island that Columbus named *San Salvador.* after traveling a distance of 8,381km (not 3,860km as he expected). Columbus thought he had reached India from the West, and so, named the group of islands he discovered, the West Indies.

On his return voyage, the Niña was forced to stop in Lisbon, Portugal, for repairs, where Columbus quickly sent note to the Spanish Court that he had successfully found a sea route to the Indies and claimed the islands there for Spain.

News about the discovery spread quickly, and Queen Isabella ordered the letter to be copied and distributed throughout the land.

When his ships finally arrived, Columbus was Spain's grandest hero.

Columbus brought with him along with natives of the islands he had found, cocoa and coffee beans, tobacco, tropical fruits, colorful birds, and precious stones (emeralds, rubies and gold), all proving his discovery of the route to the West Indies, and that the Earth was unquestionably spherical.

The Royals were extremely happy with their return on investment; Columbus had brought them the promise and hope that they longed for to save their country from economic ruination; so they set a fabulous banquet in his honor.

It is said that during this banquet, a prince spoke out to Columbus, *"Even if you had not discovered the Indies, there would have been, here in Spain which is a country abundant with great men knowledgeable in cosmography and literature, one who could have started a similar adventure with the same result."*

Columbus did not immediately respond to these words, but rather asked for a whole egg to be brought to him. He placed it on the table and said: *"My lords, I will lay a wager with any of you that you are unable to make this egg stand on its end like I will without any kind of help or aid."*

One by one, they all tried without success, and when the egg returned to Columbus, he tapped it gently on the table breaking it slightly and, with this, the egg stood on its end.

All those present then understood what he meant: that once the feat has been done, anyone knows how to do it.

Columbus then responded to the prince (something along these lines): *"You are right, any man knowledgeable in cosmography and literature could have started a similar adventure of discovery, but they didn't and I did; nobody dared to undertake this voyage into the unknown, but I did, I took on this enormous venture, I discovered the Indies, and so, its glory is mine."*

The Takeaway: *You will note how many times Columbus attempted over a period of 7 years to get backing from the various monarchs of Europe for his voyage (1485-1492), until he eventually succeeded in securing one. One can but* *say that Columbus strongly believed in his purpose, was very persistent, had positive attitude, high self-confidence and great courage, all of which point towards achieving success.*

"Fame and glory belong to those who are the first to achieve things, not those who only think about it or do it after it's been done."

- Nabil N. Jamal

Churchill's "Nevers"

Source: *Several sources on the internet and Wikipedia.*

Winston Churchill (1874-1965), was a prominent UK political leader, twice Prime Minister, and one of the great wartime leaders of World War II.

On October 29, 1941, then Prime Minister Winston Churchill was invited to speak at the graduation ceremony at his old school, Harrow.

Churchill was the leader who brought his people hope with his rock solid stand in defiance of the continuous German Air force bombardment of England.

The graduates received him with a joyous uproar; and as soon as they quieted down, Churchill paused for a moment of silence as he veered the graduates, then said,

"Never, ever, ever, ever, ever, ever, ever, give in.
Never give in. Never give in. Never give in."

Then he sat down.

The above speech became one of Churchill's most quoted, but it was subject to distortion, which eventually became more popular than the original and his most motivational, as.. *"Never, never, never, never give-up."*

The Takeaway*: Never give up on anything that you do with conviction, no matter how much hardship you face, or how strong your competition - even if your implements are few, but you continue to think positively, you will ultimately find means to prevail.*

*"The only instance where **five** purely **negative** words have had such a highly **positive** motivational impact are Winston Churchill's, "Never, never, never, never give-up."*

- Nabil N. Jamal

Ping-Pong Balls

In 1964, the freighter *"Al Kuwait"* sank in Kuwait Harbor, with a cargo of 6,000 sheep. This harbor also contained the main desalination plant that feeds drinking water to the entire city. There were immediate concerns, if the sheep carcasses were left to rot inside the ship, and eventually float into the water intake of the desalination plant, it would lead to an environmental disaster. It was vital that the ship be floated to the surface without breaking its hull to prevent the carcasses from breaking free.

The Kuwaiti government studied the emergency with several specialists in marine recovery, and the solution presented by a Danish engineer, *Karl Kroyer* was chosen. Kroyer's solution was simple; he injected 27 million Ping-Pong balls into the hold of the *Al Kuwait*, and easily raised her whole without damaging its hull.

When Kroyer was asked how he came up with this ingenious idea, he answered it was not his at all, that he had adopted it from a *Walt Disney's Donald Duck* comic book, where Donald's boat had sunk, and he pumped Ping-Pong balls to raise it to the surface.

Today, Kroyer's method is a staple in marine salvage operations.

The Takeaway: *Sometimes an absurdly simple idea is the solution to a complex issue as in this story. You never know where or how you'll find inspiration to solve a problem; but to improve your chances of inspiration, consider all options, read a lot - in various subjects, watch scientific discoveries in the TV News, explore any source that helps you widen your scope of knowledge, think out of the box, creatively, differently from others, then your unique solution may hit you, and you will shine above the rest.*

Cargo Ship Set to Sail

For thousands of years, before engines were installed in ships, ships relied on their sails to voyage with their cargo across the seas.

In the mid-20th Century, a dhow (an Indian sail ship) arrives at Dubai Sea Port carrying goods from India. The harbor master instructs the ship's captain to throw his rope to tie his ship to a docking pod on the port floor. The captain orders his crew to drop anchor, and lower the sails.

The ship then empties its cargo (cotton products, herbs, spices, tea, rice, etc.) on the port floor - so as to transport them to the city and trade with them.

A few days later, the ship is reloaded with cargo that it would carry back to India.

Consider the following four related scenarios that follow in sequence:

a) If the captain and crew board the ship, but the rope is still tied to the docking pod, can this ship sail? The answer is No.

b) If we now untie the rope from the docking pod, can this ship sail? The answer is No, because it is still anchored.

c) If we now raise the anchor, can this ship sail? Again No, because the sails have not been raised.

d) If we now raise the sails but there is no wind, can this ship sail? Again No, without wind blowing in the sails, the ship wouldn't budge.

e) If now the wind is blowing into the sails, can this ship sail? This time the answer is yes, because everything is favorable for the ship to sail - the captain to direct the ship, the crew to steer it, the sails to trap the wind, and no anchor or rope to hold it back.

The Takeaway*: If you want to "sail" on any important action, the following interpretation of the above story helps to put your steps in perspective:*

a) *Captain and crew must be on board - you and whoever is involved in your project must take charge of the ship - the anticipated action.*

b) *Untie the rope from the pod - get rid of <u>other people's negative influences</u> because they hold you back.*

c) *Raise the anchor - get rid of your self-imposed limitations - your assumptions that you are incapable of achieving your purpose.*

d) *Raise the sails - expect to use external factors that help advance your quest.*

e) *When the wind blows, trap it in your sails - don't let fleeting opportunities pass you by, exploit them to the max to achieve your quest.*

An Eagle's Rebirth

Source: *The Internet. This article is a myth.*

The American Bald Eagle has the longest life-span of its species. It can live up to 70 years; but to reach that age, it has to *reinvent* itself.

In its 40's, its long talons weaken; they lose sharpness, and heavy prey would slip from its grip. Also, its sharp beak loses sharpness that it becomes difficult to rip open its prey's flesh and eat. But the eagle's suffering doesn't end here, its wing feathers thicken with age; they become heavier, making it harder to fly long distances without getting tired, especially when carrying its prey.

At this point, the American Bald Eagle has to decide, either (a) to take no action about its deteriorating situation and soon die because it cannot fend for itself, or (b) take some drastic measures to survive. If it opts for living longer, it starts a *painful* process of change that lasts *almost 4 months*.

It flies to a high mountain top and nests there to start its transformation process.

And for the next four months, while it is defenseless and cannot fend for itself, younger Bald Eagles provide it with food and protection from predators.

It then starts!

It files its *beak* on a smooth rock to sharpen it.

While fixing its beak, it also works on its *talons*; it files them too on rocks to sharpen them.

With its beak and talons now sharp again, the eagle plucks away its heavy wing feathers and waits for their replacements to grow!

After nearly 120 days, the American Bald Eagle takes it's famous flight of rebirth.. and *lives for 30 more years.*

The Takeaway*: The sole purpose of this article is to encourage and strengthen people. There may come a time that in order to survive, we need to go through a process of change to reinvent ourselves to what is more suitable for us for the current times.*

For example, in today's fast-pace work demands, our working sons and daughters don't have the time to visit as often as we would like them to. Having to learn how to use video conferencing on a computer becomes a must if grandparents wish to stay visually in contact with their loved ones.

Lincoln's Many Failures

The majority of Americans agree that their 16th President, Abraham Lincoln was the greatest in the history of the United States.

Yet, in his life, Lincoln faced several serious failures.

At 21.. failed in commerce.

At 22.. lost election for a legislative position.

At 22.. failed in commerce again.

At 24.. failed in commerce a third time.

At 34.. lost election to U.S. Congress.

At 36.. lost election to Congress again.

At 45.. lost election to Senate.

At 47.. lost election to U.S. Vice Presidency.

At 49.. lost election to Senate again.

At 52.. elected President of United States.

__The Takeaway__: Lincoln never gave up trying after each failure, he learned from each failure and tried again differently. Yes, failure really hurts, but it also really helps. What's very important is that you find the cause of failure and learn __not__ to repeat it; that you do not use your one or *several failures as an excuse to give up, but that you change your method after each failure, and remain confident to keep trying again, and again, and again, until you eventually succeed.*

> *"Without knowing failure how can we know we success?"*
>
> *- Nabil N. Jamal*

Japan's Post-WWII Goals

Source: *Researched from several sources on the internet, and put together by the author. The dates specified may not be very accurate, but they are within the period mentioned.*

Many people say that it is useless to work on goals because you never achieve them. Read on, this is a great true story that might positively influence your views on the subject.

World War II ended on Sep. 2, 1945 with the immediate surrender of Japan after the United States dropped two atomic bombs on the industrial cities of Hiroshima and

Nagasaki, which were the production centers of Japan's war machine (ships, planes, etc.).

The Supreme Commander of the Allied Forces, General Douglas MacArthur had insisted that the document, *'Japan's Instrument of Surrender'* be signed on board the USS Missouri, which docked in Tokyo Bay on that day for the event.

America then began its defamatory campaign that Japanese products were unreliable and of poorer quality if compared to corresponding American products; and America did succeed for a long time in its campaign, but the fact of the matter was to the contrary.

Then in 1946 *(as I mentioned in the beginning, dates may not be very accurate)*, Emperor Hirohito met with Japan's senior industrialists and stated that unless they take crucial action steps to fight this defamation, globally, it will continue to hurt Japan's economy and industries for generations. So the industrialists came up with decimal (10-year) goals to be applied on all levels of their industrial machine (procurement, production, management decisions, marketing, and sales).

The first decimal goal was that by 1955, Japan would become No. 1 worldwide in the production of fabric textiles. It succeeded but a bit later than deadline, by 1959 Japan's *Teijin Company* ranked 1st in the world in the sale of fabrics.

The second decimal goal was to become the world's largest exporter of steel by 1965. Japan had to import the raw material (iron ore) as well as its incendiary (coal); it had to rebuild its factories, produce high quality steel, and export it to global markets at cheaper than market price, in order to be able to sell it; and indeed, by 1965, *Nippon Steel* achieved its goal and became the No. 1 global exporter of steel, beating both American steel giants, Bethlehem Steel and US Steel.

The third decimal goal was to become the largest manufacturer and exporter of cars globally by 1975. Japan failed to achieve that goal as scheduled; it took an extra year to achieve it. And in 1976, Japan ranked first in the world in the production and export of cars, and it still retains this prestige to this day.

The fourth decimal goal was to become the world's largest and best electronics manufacturers by 1985. They achieved it, smashing the defamation by America permanently. Names like Canon, Casio, Seiko, Citizen, and many others became best sellers worldwide.

I remember that for a statistics course that I was taking at the American University of Beirut in the late 70's, we needed to buy a scientific calculator. It was then that I bought my first Casio scientific calculator, when the professor was recommending only American brands, TI (Texas Instruments) and HP (Hewlett Packard) "because of their reliability and accuracy". Casio had exactly the same functions and accuracy as its American counterparts, and was built to resist drops and shocks whereas TI and HP weren't. Casio was also at one-third the price of TI or HP. Within my 3 years at that university, almost all students who needed scientific calculators had shifted to either Casio or Citizen Brands.

The fifth decimal goal was to become the world's greatest exporter of laptop computers by 1995; and *Toshiba and Sony* met that deadline by outselling all American brands in that period.

The sixth decimal goal was to become the greatest robotics manufacturers in the world, as well as the most robotized heavy industries. Japan actually achieved that goal in 2001, four years before deadline, achieving extremely high quality in their finished products.

The Takeaway*: If Japan's immense goals involved all its people working in industries to work hand in hand, across all corporate hierarchies, so as to achieve their country's decimal goals, do you believe that you, a single person, are capable of setting one goal of your own, one that you will be seriously ready to work on and achieve?*

China, Korea and several other countries are now working on their own decimal goals, and you can see their successful products everywhere.

I hope the above story strengthens your belief in your capabilities and drives you to set your own goals and really work on achieving them.

Pearls

Source: *the Internet-based on true events*

In the mid-twentieth century, in a small town in France, Patrique, a talented young painter, decided to marry his love Sophie and to move to live in Paris, because everyone who saw his paintings expected a bright future for him and advised him to make the move to the Capital.

The couple settled in a small apartment in Paris; their ambitions were clear from the beginning, he would become a great painter and she a famous writer.

In the neighborhood where they lived, Sophie befriended a nice, wealthy lady who one day, lent Sophie her pearl necklace to wear at a wedding in her town, asking only that she took good care of it.

Upon returning to Paris, Sophie discovered that she had lost the necklace, and after searching hopelessly, she burst into tears, as did Patrique who felt the pain of this embarrassing situation. They decided to buy a new necklace, exactly like the one Sophie had lost, to give back to the old lady without letting her know what had happened.

To achieve this, they sold all their belongings and took a staggering loan with an obscenely high interest rate. They then bought an identical pearl necklace, and presented it to the old lady who never suspected that it was a different one.

The large loan obliged them to leave their apartment and move into a small room in the slums.

To pay off the debt, Sophie abandoned her dream of becoming a writer, and started working as a housemaid; and Patrique stopped painting and became a porter in the airport. They stayed liked this for 25 years, their dreams dead and their ambitions lost.

One day, while shopping for vegetables for the home where she worked, Sophie met by chance her rich old friend who had lent her the pearl necklace.

 - What happened to you, Sophie? You look in a sorry state. Why did you and your husband disappear all of a sudden?

- Do you remember Madame, the precious pearl necklace that you had lent me to attend a wedding in my village? Well, I had lost it; and so we were obliged to buy you a new, expensive one to replace it, and the interest on the loan we took, well, we are still paying it to this day.

- Mon Dieu! (Oh, my God) Why didn't you tell me Sophie? My necklace was a fake, not real pearls, not worth five francs!

The Takeaway: *Our fear, dignity and pride may sometimes prevent us from communicating our mistakes to those involved; we may tend to hide what went wrong and take hasty actions that may prove catastrophic, as in this story; all because we avoid communicating the truth. I am not saying that by communicating the truth to those involved you will be absolved of your mistakes; you will still be obliged to fix them, but at least the burden of hiding the mistakes from them will be gone, and the repair process will definitely feel a bit lighter on your shoulders.*

4ft, 8.5in

Source: *The Internet; submitted by my brother Sany N. Jamal, a renowned Lebanese architect.*

The U.S. standard railroad gauge (distance between the rails) is 4ft, 8.5in, a rather odd number.

By utilizing the "5 Whys" *(a problem-analysis technique that determines the root cause of a problem)*, the source was able to identify how this odd number, 4ft, 8.5in came to be used today by the US railroad system. Here's how the "5 Whys" technique was used in this study.

1. *Why was this specific gauge used?*
   Because that's the way they built them in England, and the English designed the first railroads in the United States.

2. *Why did the English build them like that?*
   Because their first railroads were based on the pre-railroad tramways; tramway tracks had that same wheel-spacing as the channels used earlier by wagons.

3. *Why did wagons have that particularly odd wheel-spacing?*
   Because some of the old, long distance roads in England had *grooves* of this size in them; a different wheel-spacing would cause them to break on those old roads if they did not fit in the grooves.

4. *Why did "England" have such grooves in its old roads?*
Imperial Rome built the first long distance roads in Europe (including England). Their army chariots had that specific wheel spacing, and they formed the initial grooves in the roads which everyone else had to match for fear of breaking their wheels. Those roads have been used ever since, modified, but still in use.

5. *Why this spacing between Roman chariot wheels?*
Roman army chariots were built just wide enough to fit the rear ends of two horses (two horses' behinds).

Summation: The U.S. standard railroad gauge is the same as that of the English 4ft, 8.5in, which in turn is based on the ancient Roman chariot width measuring 2 horses' backsides.

Problem: A Space Shuttle sitting on its launch pad has two big SRBs (solid rocket boosters) attached to the sides of its main fuel tank. They are made at a factory in Utah, and have to be shipped by train from that factory to the launch site.

But the railroad from the factory runs through an old tunnel, slightly wider than the old railroad track - a bit wider than two horses' behinds, and the SRBs had to pass through that tunnel.

So the design of the SRB, a major space shuttle element, had to take into consideration its passage through this tunnel whose track width was set *three thousand years ago!*

How come the U.S. standard railroad gauge was never changed?

The answer is simple and applicable everywhere (not just the USA) → Bureaucracy!

The Takeaway: Not everything that was doable and justified in the past is necessarily doable and justified today. We need to check on the feasibility of our old methods and update them if necessary to suit what is needed today.

Utilizing the "5 Whys" technique when something doesn't seem right, helps us dig more into the matter and find its core cause. Thereafter, if a change is necessary, we would need to think on how to implement that change.

Two Crabs

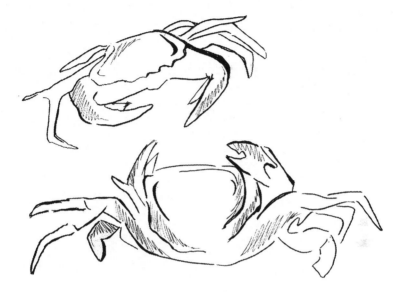

A fable by *Aesop*

One fine day, two Crabs came out from their hole to take a stroll on the sandy shore.

"My son," said the mother, *"you are walking very awkwardly; you should adjust your movement to walking straight ahead instead of sideways."*

Dear mother," replied her son, *"Do please show me how, and I will do like you."*

__The Takeaway__: Leaders should set an example by first applying their ways to themselves before preaching it to their followers, for how can you expect them to do as you want if you are incapable of doing it yourself?

An ancient Arab proverb: If you want to be obeyed ask for what is possible.

Three Stone Masons

Source: *The internet*

Michelangelo Buonarroti is the great 15th Century Italian sculptor, painter, architect and engineer, who was responsible for some of the greatest statues and paintings in all history including the great Sistina chapel in the Vatican.

One day as Michelangelo was buying marble from a rock quarry, he came upon three stone masons who were working at shaping square rocks from large blocks of marble.

His curiosity drove him to ask what each of them thought he was doing with his rock.

The *first* mason who was hammering at his rock, said: *"Can't you see? I am cutting a stupid rock!"*

The *second* mason who was carefully chiseling his rock, said: "*I am cutting this block of rock and making sure that it is per the specifications I was given, because it must fit perfectly in a wall.*"

The *third* mason, who was passionately carving his rock and smiling, said: "*I am building a great cathedral!*"

The three masons were doing exactly the same job, but each gave a very different answer based on his attitude, the most noteworthy being that of the third.

__The Takeaway__: Why was the third mason's answer so significant? He saw the final picture and the importance of his contribution beyond the obvious; that placing his quality blocks in the cathedral's walls and columns was a legacy he was leaving behind for all future generations to admire; and this made him feel very good with himself.

I know that I am leaving a legacy behind, are you? Are you dealing with your family and coworkers in a way that they will admire and remember you for it? Or like that first stone mason, you just don't care what others think of you?

People will invariably remember both, your good and bad intentions and actions, and they will judge you by them. If you do care to leave a positive legacy behind, don't delay, make amends with them now; start showing them a more likeable you with positive actions that stand-out, ones that they will always remember; and please, do it while you still can.

Bundle of Sticks

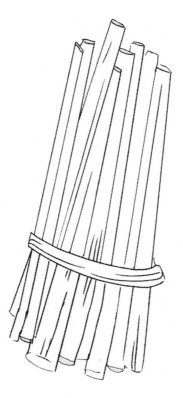

A Biblical story

Over three thousand years ago, a farmer called his four sons to his deathbed to pass his inheritance on to them.

He presented them with a bundle of wooden sticks, and said that he who breaks all them shall head the family after he's gone and inherit everything, the land, the sheep, and the house.

At first, the eldest smiled thinking it too simple, but as much as he tried bending the bundle, he failed; then the second, third and fourth sons, in turn, all tried, with no success. They then turned to their father wondering who can inherit the land if none could break the bundle.

The father asked for the bundle back, and proceeded to pull out one stick at a time and break it, until he broke them all.

He then said: "*Our land is fertile and we have a big herd, and many tribes will try to take them away from you. This means there will be war; to win against all of them..*

a. *Divide and conquer! Separate each of your enemies from the rest - just like pulling out one wooden stick out of the bundle; that way you can defeat each of them alone.*

b. *At the same time, the four of you must always stand together as one. Strong as this wooden bundle no one can break you; but should you break up with one another, your enemies will isolate and defeat each of you separately.*

c. *Stay together as one, and separate them; do it this way, and you will win all your battles.*"

In case you were wondering, the above three points are the Takeaway *of this story.*

On Thin Ice

One cold winter afternoon, a man's car broke down on a road not far from a frozen river. He saw that there was a town across the river, and so started walking towards it. As he arrived at the river bank, he saw that there was no bridge in sight, and he needed to cross while there was still enough light to see, and before the weather becomes freezing cold.

How thick was the ice? Could it hold his weight? After much hesitation, he got down on his hands and knees and began to crawl across the ice, hoping that by distributing his body weight to his hands and knees there would be less chance of the ice breaking under him.

An hour later, as it was starting to get dark, and having crawled more than halfway across the river, he heard singing coming up from behind him. He slowly turned his head to see a truck loaded with timber starting to cross the frozen river; its driver singing cheerfully, and with no hesitation whatsoever, passed the crawling man and crossed to the other bank of the river.

Here was this crawler, and there, that much heavier "truck" that crossed the same ice-covered river quickly and confidently!

What a strange sight it must have been for the truck driver to see someone crawling across the river. What a shock for the crawler, fearfully distributing his weight on his hands and knees, to see someone with a much heavier load cross the river so confidently, so quickly.

The Takeaway*: This story illustrates how many of us live our lives. I categorize people in this frozen river scenario as follows:*

i.   *Bankers: People who stand on the banks of no-risk; they never venture on untested ground.*

ii. *Crossers: Two types..*

    a) *Crawlers - those who very cautiously attempt something that they haven't experienced before because they have no choice - the situation demands them to do it (in this story, the man was obliged to cross so as not to freeze on the road at night). Such people crawl, not walk, because they fear the unknown (the strength of the ice).*

b) *Followers - those who are ready to do things once they know that somebody else has done it before them. (This man, having seen the heavy truck cross confidently, would have now surely stood up and walked across the ice.)*

iii. *Movers: People who dare and cross; their confidence inspires others to follow, just like this trucker.*

Spending one's life in doubt and fear surely isn't very healthy, and yet so many people have been influenced to live that way, low key, out of harm's way by one or many possible factors, to name a few.

- *Over-protective parents who are afraid that their children may hurt themselves if they are allowed to experience things on their own.*
- *A shy childhood that didn't allow for much interaction with other children of the same gender and age. Again, the reason is the parent's over-protection.*
- *A past experience that really hurt, and taught you negatively not to do <u>anything</u> that you might regret.*
- *No interaction with confident, daring people.*

But if it matters to you not to be labeled "banker", "crawler" or "follower", you need to encourage yourself to try crossing the ice on your own - so just stand up and start.

The Show off Archer

Source: *Ou Yang Wen Zhong Gong, Chinese Thinker (ca 1000A.D.)*

During the Northern Song Dynasty in China, there was a great young archer named Chen Yaozi. Chen loved to draw a big crowd to show-off his mastery of archery, and they would applaud him on his skill.

And yet, one day while the crowd was applauding him, he noticed that an old man did not. So he asked the old man why he did not applaud him, was he a better archer?

The old man quietly pulled out a hollow copper coin from his pocket and put it on the mouth of a bottle.

He then poured oil from a height through the small hole of the coin into the bottle without a drop touching the coin at all.

Chen was amazed at the old man's great hidden skill.

The old man said modestly: "What I have shown you is just a skill that I gained by doing hundreds of times."

Chen Yaozi understood the old man's message; and from that day on, he practiced his archery without showing-off in front of crowds.

The Takeaway: Skills are acquired by practice, and everybody has one or more skills to be proud of, but not everyone shows them off. For example, a neurosurgeon shows his skill in the operating room, a lawyer demonstrates his in court; each of them is very skilled in what he does, but neither can do the other's job. Also, not everyone cares to be a neurosurgeon or a lawyer, more proof that we become skillful at what we like. The lesson here is to show your skill but not to show it off.

Blind Men Crossing

Source: *George Shearing, jazz pianist*

A blind man had been waiting a while at a busy road for someone to help him cross to the other side, when he felt a tap on his shoulder.

"Excuse me, Sir," said the tapper, *"I'm blind - would you mind guiding me across the road?"*

The first blind man took the arm of the second blind man, and they both crossed the road. The first blind man was the famous jazz pianist, George Shearing, himself, who after that event said, *"What could I do? I took him across and it was the biggest thrill of my life."*

The Takeaway*: There are times when we wrongly think that we are incapable of a specific action and so do not risk trying it; and yet being forced to take certain risks can often help us reduce our dependencies on others, overcome personal fears, and find excitement in our newly-discovered capabilities.*

Other Side of the Picture

Source: *various on the internet*

A man was trying to read a serious article in his newspaper after returning home from work, but his little daughter was constantly interrupting his concentration because she wanted him to play with her.

In an attempt to occupy her away from him, he ripped a page from the newspaper that had the map of the world printed on it, and tore the map into small pieces. He then gave it to his daughter and asked her to go to her room and paste the parts of map together correctly, then bring it back for him to see; thinking that it would take her all day to do it, as being so young, she wouldn't know geography.

But the child returned within minutes with the correctly completed map, to her father's total surprise.

When he asked how she managed to get it right so fast, she replied: *"There was a photo of a man on the other side of the paper; I worked on getting the man's photo right, so as to get the map right."*

Then she ran to out to play alone in the garden, leaving her father stunned with her solution.

The Takeaway: There is always another side to all that you face in life. Whenever you encounter a challenging situation, look at it from another angle (a different perspective), and you may be happily surprised to find a solution to that problem - one that you have not thought of before.

Sometimes our minds get clouded with thoughts that prevent us from thinking straight. The solution to this is simple:

a) *Go do something else, preferably out of the office or home. Occupying yourself for some time with something else will clear your mind from all thoughts on the problem.*

b) *Now go back to the problem with a clear mind, you will be able to see things much clearer, because you've emptied all cloudiness from your mind. Your chances of finding a solution are much better when you now look at the problem fresh, from zero.*

Shoes

Source: *Based on Ken Burnett's blog: The Bata Shoes Story*

At the end of the Nineteenth century, several English shoe manufacturers sent their sales representatives to colonial Africa to investigate and report back if it was feasible to market their shoes there.

All representatives made the same observation, *"Nobody wears shoes in Africa."* and their conclusions were also similar, *"We are wasting our time, there is no market for our shoes here."*

All of them, except for the BATA Shoes representative. He made the same observation as all the rest, *"Nobody wears shoes in Africa."* but his conclusion was refreshingly positive, *"Wow! I can see massive sales potential for our shoes here!"*

And that is why signs promoting BATA appear all over Africa, even in the remotest of spots. It is also why BATA's shoes are known as the shoes of Africa.

The Takeaway: While all other representatives saw only negatives, problems and a waste of time, the positive mindset of the BATA representative let him see the opportunity of being the first to dress African feet with shoes.

Differences in the interpretation of facts are highly affected by one's attitude towards the subject, past experiences, likes and dislikes, motivations, mood, and personal interest, all of which can seriously influence how a company directs its efforts.

When companies base their decisions on personal conclusions and not the facts alone, and when they heed negative mindsets rather those positive, chances are they will take wrong decisions.

> *"It is always better to look at a matter positively before ruling negatively on it."*
> — Nabil N. Jamal

Fresh Fish

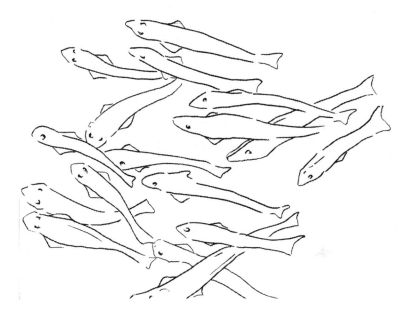

Source: *the Internet, presented by Rosette Nuwaysir*

The Japanese eat a lot of fresh fish.

Over decades of excessive fishing habits, the fish in the Sea of Japan have eventually, and permanently migrated to distant areas.

And so, Japanese fishing boats got bigger and went farther than ever. The farther the fishermen went, the longer it took to bring in the fish. If the return trip took more than a few days, the fish would not arrive fresh, and the Japanese would not buy them.

FREEZERS: To solve this problem, fishing companies installed freezers on their boats. They would catch the fish and freeze them at sea. Freezers allowed the boats to go farther and stay longer. However, the Japanese could distinguish between fresh and frozen fish, and they did not like frozen fish.

LIVE FISH TANKS: So, the Japanese fishing companies installed fish tanks on their boats. They would catch the fish and stuff them into the tanks, fin to fin. After a little thrashing around, the fish would stop moving; and arrived tired and dull. But the Japanese people could still taste the difference. Because the fish did not move for days, they lost their fresh-fish taste. The Japanese preferred the lively taste of fresh fish, not sluggish fish.

So how did Japanese fishing companies eventually overcome this problem? How do they get fresh-tasting fish to Japan?

SHARK IN THE TANK: To overcome this problem and deliver the fish tasting fresh, they still stuffed the fish into the tanks, but now added a motion-motivator to keep them on edge, a small shark in each tank.

The shark would eat a few fish, but in doing so, the rest of the fish are challenged to move out of the shark's way to stay alive. They arrive alert and energetic, tasting-fresh.

The Takeaway*: Many of us, like the fish, are living in a fish tank and most of the times are tired and dull. The shark in the fish tank represents new challenges that motivate us to keep productive and lively. We need a <u>shark</u> in our life, a motion-motivator to keep us energized and sharp.*

Fox and Cat

A fable by Aesop

A Fox was boasting to a Cat about the many ways he knows of to escape his enemies.

"I have only one, climbing up a tree, and it works fine for me." said the Cat.

Just at that moment, they heard the cry of a pack of hunting dogs racing towards them. The Cat immediately climbed up a tree and hid in its branches, and asked the fox laughingly, *"What are you going to do?"*.

The Fox thought first of one way, then of another, and while he was deciding on which way to use, the dogs surrounded him. The hunters soon arrived and killed the fox.

The Cat who had been looking on, said mockingly: *"Better one safe way than a hundred on which you cannot decide."*

The Takeaway:

1) *Time is precious: The Fox lost precious time in his confusion.*

2) *Grab the moment's opportunity: Both, Cat and Fox had the same opportunity to escape, the cat took it, the fox didn't.*

3) *Decide! When there are many choices, decide on one. The Fox couldn't decide on any.*

4) *Implementation: The Cat took instant action on its only way to escape; climbing the tree.*

Ethics: It's not nice to look down upon others when you manage to save your own neck and watch them suffer.

Guillotine

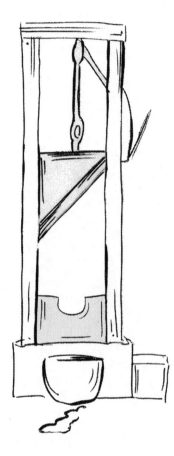

Source: *Several on the internet*

A story is told about three people, a religious man, a lawyer, and an engineer, who were sentenced to death-execution by guillotine.

The religious man was to be executed first; the executioner placed his neck under the guillotine, and asked him if he had any last words to say?

The religious man said: "God will not leave me, God will save me."

After which, the executioner released the blade, but it stopped just before touching his neck.

The witnesses cried out: "Release the religious man, God has spoken". And so, the religious man's life was spared.

Next came the lawyer's turn at the guillotine; the executioner placed his neck under the sharp blade, and asked him if he had any last words to say?

The lawyer said: "I do not know God like the religious man does, but I do know that justice will save me".

After which, the executioner released the blade, but again it stopped just before touching his neck.

The witnesses cried out: "Release the lawyer, justice has spoken". And so, his life too was spared.

Finally, it was the engineer's turn at the guillotine; the executioner placed his neck under the sharp blade, and asked if he had any last words to say?

The engineer said: "I do not know God like the religious man, or justice like the lawyer, but I do know that there is a knot in the rope of the guillotine that is preventing it from going down all the way".

The executioner examined the knot and fixed it, he then released the blade over the engineer's neck, and this time it worked perfectly!

The Takeaway: *Volunteering information generally hurts the speaker, in which case it is best not to volunteer it. In sales it may spoil the deal, example: a prospect asked a car salesman if he had the model that he liked in orange because he wanted a unique color; the salesman replied, "Yes, we have over 150 units in orange." The prospect didn't buy because he wanted a unique color; volunteering the existence of 150 units spoiled the deal for the salesman.*

Mouse Trap

A fable about caring

A mouse looked through the crack in the wall to see the farmer and his wife open a package. "*What food might this contain?*", the mouse wondered - To his shock, it was a mousetrap!

Retreating to the farmyard, the mouse proclaimed the warning, "*There is a mousetrap in the house! There is a mousetrap!*"

The chicken clucked and scratched, raised her head and said, *"Mr. Mouse, I can tell this is a grave concern to you, but it is of no consequence to me. I cannot be bothered by it."*

The mouse turned to the lamb and told him, *"There is a mousetrap in the house! There is a mousetrap!"*

The lamb sympathized, but said, *"I am so very sorry, Mr. Mouse, but there is nothing I can do about it but pray; be assured you are in my prayers."*

The mouse turned to the cow and said, *"There is a mousetrap in the house! There is a mousetrap!"*

The cow said, *"Wow, Mr. Mouse. I'm sorry for you, but it's no skin off my nose."*

And so, the mouse returned to the house, feeling miserable and disappointed with his friends' reactions, to face the farmer's mousetrap alone.

That very night, the sound of the mousetrap catching its prey was heard throughout the house. The farmer's wife rushed to see what the trap had caught, and in the darkness, she did not see that it was a poisonous snake caught by the tail, and which bit her.

The farmer rushed his wife to hospital, but she returned home with a fever. In those days, it was traditional to treat fever with fresh chicken soup; so the farmer took his hatchet to the farmyard for the soup's main ingredient, chicken!

But his wife's fever would not subside, so friends and neighbors came to sit with her around the clock. To feed them, the farmer butchered the lamb.

The farmer's wife eventually died, and many people came for her funeral. The farmer had the cow slaughtered to provide enough beef for all of them.

The mouse looked upon it all from his crack in the wall with great sadness.

The Takeaway: Whenever you hear someone that you know-family, friend, or coworker is facing a problem, and think it does not concern you, remember, when one of us is threatened, we are all at risk.

We are all involved in our various circles-family, friends, and coworkers, and we must make it a point to support one another whenever necessary, and in any way that can help reduce the frustration or pain-encouragement, moral boost, finances, and whatever else that helps.

Two Frogs in a Pit

Source: *The internet, author unknown*

<u>A group</u> of frogs was hopping through <u>the woods one day</u>, when two of them accidentally fell into a deep pit of mud.

When the other <u>frogs</u> saw how deep the pit was, they shouted to those two that it was impossible for them to get out of the pit, and that they shouldn't even bother trying because they are surely going to drown in the mud.

The two frogs ignored the comments and tried to jump and climb up out of the pit with all their might, but the other frogs repeated their shouts to stop, that it was useless, and that they were as good as dead.

Finally, one of the two gave up and drowned in the mud.

The other frog continued to jump and climb up as hard as he could until he eventually made it out of the pit. He then thanked each of the other frogs for their continued *'encouragement'*, that without it, he would have surely given up as his friend did. He added that although he did not hear their words because he was *deaf*, none-the-less, he was truly thankful for their encouraging shouts that kept him trying against all odds.

The Takeaway*: Ignore those who push you down and demotivate you; listen only to those who energize you to succeed, because encouragement gives you hope and motivates you to persist in your tries to accomplish what others see as difficult or even impossible.*

Donkey in the Well

Source: *The Internet, based on a true story*

A farmer's donkey fell into an abandoned concrete well. The fall hurt the donkey and it started to neigh out-loud, and the farmer heard its cries and came running.

The farmer could not figure out how to get his donkey out of the well, so he asked his neighbors for help; they came and assessed the situation as follows:

1. *This abandoned old well is dangerous; people could fall in it and get hurt. It must be filled and closed forever.*

2. *The donkey couldn't possibly serve its master any longer as it has been hurt by the fall.*

3. *The cost of renting a crane with pulleys to recover the donkey was more expensive than the purchase price of a new donkey.*

The farmers unanimously agreed that the most doable course of action is to forget the rescue operation and to focus on filling the well with soil to prevent anyone from falling into it; and this would mean burying the donkey alive.

They started shoveling soil into the well, but as soon as the soil started falling on the donkey's back, it realized what was happening and started crying even louder.

But before long, the donkey stopped its cries; its unexpected silence intrigued the farmers, so they looked inside the well only to see the smart donkey shaking the soil off its back onto the ground, trampling on it with its hoofs to harden it, and climb over it.

Realizing that the situation has now changed, that the donkey could be saved after all, the farmers continued throwing soil into the well, and the donkey would shake it off its back, harden it with its hoofs, and climb even higher and higher; until it was able to reach the mouth of the well, and with all its strength, and with the help of the farmers, it climbed out and ran into the field, alive and free after a terrifying ordeal.

The Takeaway*: Life is like the deep well in this story, and every problem that you face is like the soil; you must (a) loosen the soil off your back, and (b) step on it to overcome it, and (c) by doing that, you can achieve higher ground.*

- *Realize that crying in a bad situation never helps; stop crying! The donkey stopped crying and thought of a solution for his fatal problem.*

- *Plato said: "Necessity is the mother of invention". Had the donkey not thought of its own solution to get out of the well, it would have most certainly been buried alive.*

- *Always think of solutions to problems - if a donkey can do it, so can you. Keep in mind that when you overcome a problem, you develop confidence to face even tougher ones.*

- *Ask yourself the following, and answer them:*

   "How can I solve this problem?"

   "Can it be done differently; are there any other options?"

Tourist and Fishermen

Source: *The internet, based on a true story.*

An American tourist complimented the local Mexican fishermen on the quality of their fish and asked how long it took to catch them.

"Not very long." they answered.

The American tourist then asked them, *"Why didn't you stay out at sea longer and catch more fish?"*

The fishermen explained that their small catches were sufficient to meet their needs and those of their families.

He then asked, *"So what do you do with the rest of your time?"*

The replied, *"We sleep late, play with our children, dance with our wives. In the evenings, we meet with our friends, play the guitar, and sing a few songs. We have a full life."*

The tourist interrupted, *"I have an MBA from Harvard and I can help you! You should start by fishing longer every day. You can then sell the extra fish you catch. With the extra revenue, you can buy a bigger boat."*

The fishermen asked, *"And after that?"*

The tourist replied, *"With the extra money the larger boat will bring, you can buy a second and a third one, and so on until you have an entire fleet of trawlers. Instead of selling your fish to a middle man, you can then negotiate directly with the processing plants and maybe even open your own plant. You can then leave this little village and move to Mexico City, Los Angeles, or even New York City! From there you can direct your huge enterprise."*

They asked, *"How long would that take?"*

"Perhaps fifteen years." replied the tourist.

They again asked. *"And after that?"*

He replied with a smile, *"Afterwards? Well my friend, that's when it gets really interesting; when your business gets really big, you can start buying and selling stocks and make millions!"*

"Millions? Really? And after that?" asked the fishermen.

The tourist answered, *"After that you'll be able to retire, live in a tiny village near the coast, sleep late, play with your children, catch a few fish, take a siesta with your wife and spend your evenings enjoying your friends."*

"But that's exactly what we are doing now. So what's the point in wasting fifteen years?" asked the Mexicans.

The Takeaway:

1) *Know what you want in life, you may already have it.*

2) *Not everyone wants to be rich, actually you don't need to be rich to have a good life. I remember as a child asking my father while seeing poor children playing in the street, "How come they look so happy when they are so poor?" To which my father replied, "Son, the poor live a much simpler and content lives than the rich; they do not worry about money because to them a little of it is enough, unlike the rich who always want more to satisfy their fake way of living".*

3) *Some people are content with a peaceful, relaxed life.*

Two Hungry Asses

Source: *The author, Nabil N. Jamal*

A farmer who made use of his two asses in the field, tied them together with a rope when it was time for his lunch and nap.

As the hungry asses stood among two bales of hay, each pulled towards the bale closest to him to eat; but as hard as each pulled, neither prevailed.

Exhausted from their exertion, the two asses stopped pulling each other to analyze the situation: there is plenty of food, but neither is reaching it. They now saw clearly what they must do; they fed together at one bale then the other.

The Takeaway: Conflicts of interest can be resolved with teamwork and a common benefit in mind.

Chihuahua, Monkey & Leopard

Source: *the Internet, author unknown*

An explorer took her pet Chihuahua (dog) with her on an Amazon safari. Wandering too far one day, the Chihuahua got lost in the bush, and soon encountered a leopard. The Chihuahua realized that he's in trouble because of the size and muscular build of the big cat, but noticing some fresh bones on the ground, he settled to bite on them, with his back turned to the approaching leopard.

As the leopard was about to leap on the dog, the Chihuahua smacked his lips and exclaimed loudly, *"Mmm! that was a delicious leopard, I wonder if there are any more around here."*

Hearing this, the leopard immediately stopped and turned away quietly into the woods as a look of fear overcame him, saying, *"That was close! That mean dog nearly had me!!"*

Meanwhile, a monkey who had been watching the whole scenario from a nearby tree figured he can put his knowledge to good use and trade it for protection from the leopard.

The Chihuahua saw the monkey go after the leopard, and guessed that he might be up to no good.

When the leopard heard the monkey's explanation, he was enraged at being made a fool of; and offered the monkey a ride back to observe his revenge.

The Chihuahua saw them approaching and feared for the worse; but instead of running, he sat down, again with his back turned to them and pretending not to notice them; and when the pair was within hearing distance, he said loudly, *"Now where's that monkey gone? I sent him off an hour ago to bring me another leopard . . ."*

The Takeaway: *His wit, his bold bluff saved the dog twice today from disaster, but in reality, this is not a doable thing, you cannot keep on fooling people all the time.*

> *"Fool me once; fool me twice; but shame on me if you fool me thrice."*
>
> - Nabil N. Jamal

Importance of Smiling

Source: *Several, compiled by my daughter, Sarah N. Jamal for her article in our last Brain Food ezine, Vol. 3, issue 26, Feb. 2012, a portion of which is based on the documentary, "The Human Body".*

In business, your primary goal when working with a new potential client is to get them to *like* you, *trust* you and *want to listen* to you.

In face-to-face communication, people judge you during the first 15 seconds of meeting you. Most people do this subconsciously, but they try to get a *reading* of your body language from the first moment they glance at you - how you are dressed, whether you walk with confidence, and if you are someone they would feel at ease in doing business with; and once you stand close enough to anybody, they will automatically focus on your eyes and mouth.

Most people don't even need to "think" about smiling, it just comes naturally to them; but there are those who very rarely smile. Here's a simple test, ask someone that you see every day, a family member, coworker, friend, close neighbor, anyone that you trust - how often they see you smiling; if they say, "not a lot", it's time for you to consider changing.

Another simple test is to pay attention to whether or not other people smile back at you. Smiling is actually *contagious*; if you smile at someone, chances are that they'll smile back, or in the very least their stiff facial expressions will soften; but if you don't see a change in that person's facial expressions, it means you are either not smiling enough, or not too sincerely.

Political smile: The Hon. Dame Margaret Thatcher, Ex-Prime Minister of the UK, (nicknamed: the Iron Lady) is a great example of political smiling. Ms. Thatcher invariably exploited smiling throughout her political life to achieve her goals.

In 1982, when Argentina invaded and grabbed the British Falkland Islands, Ms. Thatcher was intent on regaining them. When diplomatic pressure and negotiations led to nowhere, Ms. Thatcher asked her greatest ally, US President Ronald Reagan (with whom she had an exceptionally strong political alliance) to look *the other way* as she was about to wage war. She then sent a combined SAS and Navy strike force to eject the invaders. She won! she regained the Falklands, and in doing so, toppled the Argentine government, and had its president deposed and court martialed for taking his country to war. The Iron Lady's popularity grew immensely, at home and all over the world.

Ms. Thatcher had exploited her smile first to sell the idea of having to go to war to the British public while expressing her confidence in winning it. After the war was won, she also used her smile when addressing the Argentinian people to express her noble intentions towards them.

Japanese culture and smiling: In the not too distant past, smiling was not acceptable in Japanese culture, actually, it was considered shameful to smile. Women would shave their eyebrows, and re-draw them much higher on their foreheads so as not to show their facial expressions of happiness. To this very day, we still see that when some Japanese women smile, they would raise a hand to cover their smile, because their culture does not promote smiling or showing one's teeth.

Ever since WWII, the western way of living has clearly influenced Japanese lifestyles. Japanese research has recently shown that as a direct result of smiling to clients, chances of closing sales deals increase by <u>30-50%</u>. Ever since then, most Japanese corporations have been conducting in-house professional smiling classes for their sales and customer service teams in order to develop a more natural-looking smile; the older generation of staff had a harder time accommodating smiling because as mentioned earlier, their culture didn't allow for it. To help them smile, they were asked to practice biting on chopsticks; in doing so, their cheek muscles would recede and show a facial expression of smiling.

The Takeaway: *Always try to smile because its personal benefits are many:*

- *Smiling make you feel happy, and this changes your mood, reduces your stress level, lowers your blood pressure, and boosts your immune system.*

- *Smiling is contagious; it can make others smile back at you.*

- *Smiling helps "you" stay positive, and this in turn increases your positive affect on others, and reinforces their positive perception of you.*

- *Finally, smiling lifts your cheek muscles and makes you look "younger".*

A Lesson in Failing a Whole Class

Source: *Internet*

An economics teacher recently made a statement that he had never failed a single student before, but that he had recently failed a whole class. That class had insisted that *Socialism* worked, that no one would be poor and no one would be rich, and that it is a great equaliser of people.

The teacher then said, *"To better express socialism, we will conduct an experiment of 3 tests in this class, and substitute grades for wages. I will average the class grades and each one of you will receive that same grade. This way no one will fail, but also no one will receive an "A". This is as close to socialism as you can get, and more readily understood by all of you."*

After the first test, the grades were averaged, and everyone got a "B-". The students who studied hard were upset, and those who studied little were smiling.

As the second test rolled around, the students who studied little, studied even less, and the ones who studied hard in the past, decided that they wanted a free ride too, so they studied little. The second test average was a "D". No one was happy.

When the third test rolled around, the average was an "F". Everyone failed.

The teacher then explained how the experiment of averaging their grades represented socialism, and how it would also ultimately fail with time - because when a financial reward is given to those who work for it, their efforts to succeed and earn that reward would be great; but if the government stops rewarding for effort, and everyone gets equal wages (whether they work hard or don't work at all), then nobody would want to work if they will receive their wages anyway. It could NOT be any simpler than that.

The Takeaway: To work hard or to be lazy at work are matters of attitude. If we justify giving a lazy person something that a passionate person worked hard for, why should the passionate person continue to work with enthusiasm if "by not working" he gets the same result as a lazy person?

To fix such a scenario, there must be a "differentiating" reward given to those who perform their duties well, to encourage them to continue producing with the same enthusiasm.

Legend Outside His Country

Source: *The movie, "Searching for Sugarman", the true story of Sixto Rodríguez, singer.*

For 28 years, American, Sixto Rodríguez had no knowledge that his 1970 record album, *Cold Fact* was actually more popular than The Beatles' *Abbey Road* in South Africa and Australia, and that he had become a legend in those far away countries; and yet, in his own country, the United States, he was unknown.

In the early 1970's South Africa was a police state-authoritarian, conservative and repressive. Television did not yet exist there because the government believed it to have a morally corrupting influence. Rodríguez's songs, speaking out against political repression, related strongly to the people of South Africa, who would share bootlegged cassettes of his songs, and it spread that way. Rumors of his committing suicide while performing in a concert in 1970, added the final touch to his legend.

Meanwhile, having not succeeded in music in the States, Rodríguez had been working for over two decades on construction sites, erecting and demolishing buildings for a living.

His legend in South Africa had remained completely unknown to him until 1998, when his eldest daughter accidentally came across a website dedicated to him. She contacted the website authors, and advised them that her father was still alive. The website authors then immediately traveled to Detroit and met him, and told him about his legendary status in their country and in Australia. Sixto just couldn't believe it. Upon returning to South Africa, the website authors set up a big concert for him, *"Dead Men Don't Tour: Rodríguez in South Africa 1998"*, and reissued his album *Cold Fact* on CD, which then sold platinum in South Africa, and a five-time platinum in Australia.

His musical career now brought back to life, Sixto then toured South Africa and Australia several times with much success.

In 2012, an Academy Award winning documentary film on his discovery and comeback, *"Searching for Sugar Man"*, finally gave Sixto the fame he yearned for in the United States.

The Takeaway:

> *"There is only one direction, and it is forward; it's never too early or too late."*
>
> - Sixto Rodríguez

You Can Do It, Boy!

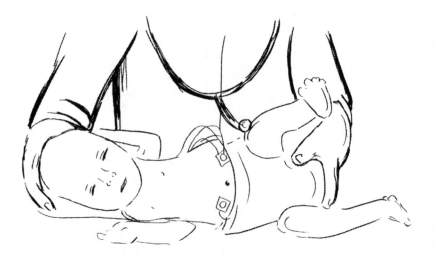

Source: *Several sources on the Internet, a true story.*

David Lofchick was born with *Spastic Cerebral Palsy* (a condition causing stiff muscles, which interferes with walking, movement and speech). David had no motor connections to the right side of his brain. There was simply nothing to do surgically, and no known cure.

Normally, we would check with one or two more doctors when we require a second medical opinion; but *Bernie Lofchick*, David's father, was well to do, and he presented his son to *thirty (30) doctors* for examination, all of whom concurred that . . .

- *David will never be able to walk,*

- *He will never be able to talk,*

- *He will never be able to count to ten,*

- *There is nothing medically possible to be done,*

- *It is better to place him in a specialized institution where he would receive special care.*

Bernie just wouldn't accept that nothing could be done to save his son from being a vegetable for the rest of his life. Until finally, when David was two, Bernie was told about a doctor, Dr. Pearlstein who was *solution-oriented,* and not *problem-conscious.*

After a thorough examination of David, Dr. Pearlstein told Bernie that his thirty colleagues were not wrong, David does have Cerebral Palsy, but all hope was not lost; that by following a very special and strict regimen, there was a very slim chance that they can make a difference in David's life, but it had to be a life-time commitment.

They would have to work with David beyond human endurance, and then push him even more. Bernie was to hire a famous physical therapist on full time basis, exclusively for this chore, and had to convert his house den into a special gym for David.

After 3 years, the physical therapist asked Bernie to come see David (now 5) perform his first push-up. It took David 10 minutes to make that one push-up, and in the process got his whole body covered with sweat from performing this one ordeal. This was the changing point in David's life.

by David's *13*th *birthday, he . . .*

- *was doing 1,100 push-ups a day*

- *was running 6 miles non-stop every day*

- *was on the school hockey team*

- *was the best table-tennis player in the county*

- *rode a bike*

- *had high grades in math*

- *spoke*

- *had many friends*

The Takeaway*: Had David been born a normal boy, it is doubtful he would have performed so extremely well. This great change in David's life is owed to 4 persons, namely:*

1. *Bernie, David's father for his unwavering belief that his son must lead a normal life and his persistency in finding a doctor with a positive mindset - and not listening to the negative views of 30 doctors who concurred that there was nothing medically possible to be done.*

2. *Dr. Pearlstein, for giving David's father the hope that he was longing to hear, and for putting him in contact with the right physical therapist to work on David.*

3. *The physical therapist whose extensive ongoing coaching and support of David made him achieve so much.*

4. *And finally, David himself, for pushing himself very hard and for never giving up, so as to make a difference in the way he lived.*

We need to constantly feed ourselves with Positive Affirmations and Beliefs.

From the moment little David Lofchick was able to comprehend, he carried around a cassette tape player, to which he would listen daily. It had only one message that was continuously repeating in his ears with the sole purpose of keeping him going through his hard times: "You Can Do It, Boy!"

Natural Enemies?

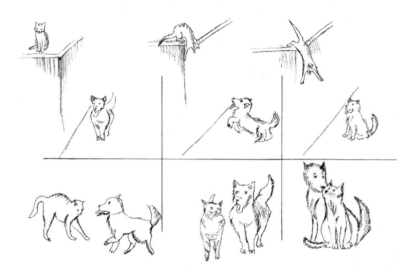

Source: *The internet*

Take a look at the sequence of sketches accompanying this story. Every day, at the same time - this cat sits on the roof waiting for that dog to arrive; the dog arrives; the cat climbs down as the dog waits patiently; they fondly greet each other by rubbing their bodies together; they go for a stroll; then the dog takes the cat back to her home, and goes to his.

They have been doing this for 5 years, and their owners did not know until neighbors seeing them together so frequently commented to the cat's owner, who then followed the dog home, quite a far distance away. How it started? No one knows.

Man's attitude towards the world surrounding him is often based on his wrong conclusions. For example, the general belief that cats and dogs are natural enemies is wrong. You can also find online many photos of cats and mice playing together.

Such photos make us question our beliefs about hostility between those animals. A cat eats mice, lizards, cockroaches and anything else smaller than its size because it is a predator and needs to hunt for food.

But if a cat has had its fill of food, it won't attack a mouse, just like tigers and crocodiles, etc.

Essentially, all species kill only for food, except for man, who in addition to killing other species for food, also kills them just for the excitement of hunting.

The Takeaway: Every now and then, it is healthy to reassess general beliefs; by reassessing them, those general beliefs are either (a) further endorsed, (b) updated to reflect a more current status, or (c) refuted by presenting convincing evidence to the contrary.